The Quantum Entanglement Party

Adventures of the Miso Mice Series
Adventures 6 - 11

Written by the Miso Mice as told to Annette Czech Kopp

ISBN: 9798395702357

Printed in the United States of America

Numbers on the bottom of pictures or at the end of a section correspond to their attributes located in the appendix. Please go to Misomice.com for the Miso Mice Characters & Lexicon Directory.

DEDICATION

I'd like to thank my husband Greg who so unconditionally and unselfishly gives me the priceless gift of beach walking and my 2 sons Nick and Bobby (Rob) who knew and named the Miso Mice a long, long time ago, and Carla and Christina……love all of you lots!!

By Annette Czech Kopp

Adventures of the Miso Mice Series:
Adventures of the Miso Mice; How It All Started and Adventures 1-5

Table of Contents

Adventure 6: The Quantum Entanglement Party 1

Adventure 7: Breakfast on the Mezzanine 9

Adventure 8: The Zodiac Girls Jewelry 16

Adventure 9: Timewalkers 23

Adventure 10: Tem-E-Laks... 27

Adventure 11: The Treasure Chest 30

Appendix: Picture Attributes 39

Adventure 6: The Quantum Entanglement Party

Time being a funny thing, the night of the party came up much more quickly than thought, and Kaame and the Miso Mice gathered on the mezzanine. "I think before we go to the party that we should sing our special song, as knowing the Zodiac Girls this party will be an adventure," suggested Suzy.

"Yes, said Polly, "that's a great idea and it offers such credibility to everything we do and now that Kaame knows it she can join in and sing with us."

"Curiosity you look great in that Vera Wang cashmere outfit! Definitely a bit different than your usual invisible suit – tres chic - very awesome! Everyone looks awesome!" added Kat. And together they danced and sang:

Open heart, open mind, for highest good, for always and in all ways.

83, 231

And then walked through the door and into the uber bizarre party which was already quite entangled! The Zodiac Girls' parties were legendary, but this time, they really outdid themselves. All kinds of things were happening everywhere and it seemed to go on forever! The happenings included: The Cat Band, spacecraft and falling star rides, a special guest appearance by the legendary sister singers "The Segments",

84, 85, 86, 87

and lots of line dancing – both horizontally and vertically – everywhere – on floors, chairs, tables, and ceilings. And yes, some attendees were wearing lampshades, but Kat said they may not have been lampshades at all but actually fashionable hats.

88, 89, 90, 91

The Earth was rocking and Fluffins of the universally renowned Weird Giraffe Games Company was hosting a tournament of their wildly popular "Way Too Many Cats" game. Of course it was a cats-only invitational and it seemed that Freddie would be the sure winner with his "lucky charm" Tappy Greenshoes sitting next to him. Gumbo the catfish was playing

too as Fluffins had decided that catfishes were actually cats in disguise, so they were invited too. During the breaks in play Gumbo had been talking to Sandman who was just watching the game, about the Rainbow Bridge, and Sandman mentioned that he was catching a ride with the Miso Mice to the bridge. Gumbo was wondering if they would give her a ride too. 92, 93

Everyone was singing, smiling, laughing and having lots of fun, thanking the Zodiac Girls and exclaiming on what an amazing party it was.

"Woo hoo! This is so cool! This looks like when we were sprites! Is this Quantum Entanglement?" asked Curiosity as she looked all around.

"Yes, this is quite beautiful. Look at all the strings of thought and other energy entangling, intersecting, and flowing through one another," added Suzy. "It looks like chaos but it's not at all."

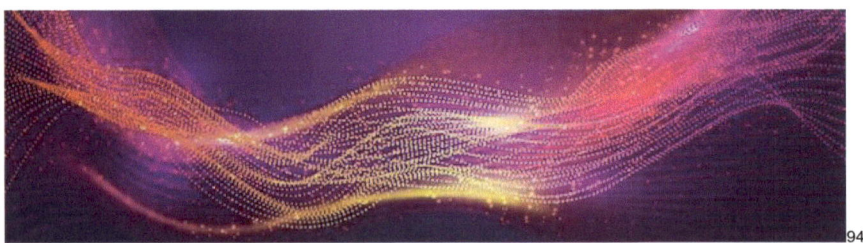

94

"I'm going to ask **PressThisButton** what Quantum Entanglement is as it does look like a mess," said Shelly. *Return to your dreams to work it out.* Quantum Entanglement is dreams and you can return to them?" asked Shelly. "How do you return to a dream? I thought dreams were over once you woke up."

"Yes silly you can return to your dreams," replied Curiosity, "My imagination is telling me that Quantum Entanglement can be anything you want, and your dreams are imagination in a different way! You can either imagine Quantum Entanglement when you are awake or asleep. Just like dreams – you can have them awake or asleep. You know 'day-dreaming'."

"And you can definitely return to a dream to work anything out. In fact, sometimes that's a really good way to figure out a problem. All you have to do is when you go to sleep at night, just ask a question – kind of like for PressThisButton but usually with dreams the answer you get includes pictures and feelings," added Suzy as she looked around.

"You can also ask the same question when you are awake and then listen to yourself for an answer, or imagine what you want the answer to be. It's that choose'ndo 2 step process," added Curiosity.

"Do you remember when you were a sprite?" Polly asked changing the subject as she walked beside Curiosity and some of the Zodiac Girls.

"Not specifically but in my imagination I do, and when I go timewalking," replied Curiosity. "But it's more of a 'knowing' thing, not a thought. Kind of like communicating without words. I just know that I was a sprite." And Kaame looked at Curiosity with a very thoughtful expression. She wanted to ask Curiosity about the 'knowing' thing but was not sure if she should do it at the party.

"That is awesome! I've only done timewalking once but it was amazing," said Kat and just then Freddie came by with Tappy Greenshoes on his back. "Oh look at that cute little doll. It has a watch on it – do you think Freddie uses it for timewalking?"

"You are absolutely right," replied Tarie. "That is Tappy Greenshoes and I'm really not sure if Tappy is a doll or not. Sometimes she looks quite lifeless and then other times you just know that she's not. I've often seen the two of them together, Tappy presses her watch or her other hand just happens to fall on her watch, they both close their eyes and when they open them again, it's like they've been to another place – classic timewalking." I'll have to ask him more about it but we've only just recently met and I'm not sure if it's something he'd like to talk about yet."

"Maybe Tappy's watch is her and Freddie's PressThisButton," posed Polly. "That could be a very credible possibility."

"I totally agree with you Polly," said Kat as she pointed to a far section of the party and asked, "What's that?"

"Some of that are the things – sprites, thoughts, ideas, etc. going along the Quantum Entanglement strings. The things have all kinds of shapes and sizes and if you come over here," explained Curiosity as she walked everyone over to another area, "You can see other examples of what they look like. Remember sprites always get to choose. I've seen all kinds of sprites in my imagination."

95, 96, 97

"I never realized that there were so many sprites and so much stuff zooming around in the Quantum Entanglement", said Polly.

"How do we get into the Quantum Entanglement?" asked Kaame. "For some reason I seem to remember something about it. I think I've experienced it," she continued as she tried to catch a feeling.

"You probably imagined it," said Curiosity, "I know I have."

"You're actually already there," Suzy answered Kaame's question. "We're already in the entanglement – we're always part of it. Up close it looks like this," Suzy continued as she pointed to the various things happening at

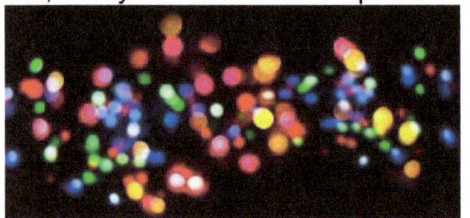

the party – The Cats Band, spacecraft and shooting star rides, line dancing, and other happenings. "But up up-in-the-universe it looks like this," and Suzy pointed to another area. "It all depends on where you are when you look at it. If you are close, you see the individual things, but if you are far, you see the general things. And like Curiosity said, and with anything, Quantum Entanglement can look like anything you want."98

"So Tarie said that Quantum Entanglement has something to do with getting the star fishes into the sky. How?" asked Shelly.

"Quantum Entanglement is how everything is linked together including choices," explained Aquie. "Once you make a choice, even if it's just a thought, it flows through the Quantum Entanglement and as **PressThisButton** answered, *The Universe will arrange the string of events to get this done in the shortest time possible*. And that's done via choos'ndo."

"But aren't you always choose'ndoing all the time?" asked Polly.

"Yes, of course, but you can also do it with awareness. You can think about what you are choosing. Be aware of what you are thinking, and focusing on. Is it really what you want? If not, then change your thinking and focus. As we've said, for some it's easier than for others. For those that want to become more aware, Suzy's techniques and exercises can help," said Tarie. 99

"I still don't get how it works. I think I need better instructions," said Shelly.

"I'm not sure if I get the whole idea at all," added Polly as she gazed around at everything.

"As I mentioned before, for some it's really simple and obvious and for others not so much so," said Tarie.

100

 "We can talk about it more later, but in the meantime, let's have some fun. I think I hear The Segments singing their smash interstellar hit "Highest Good". Anyone want to dance?"

"Wait a minute! That's our special song!" exclaimed Shelly as she listened to the melody and lyrics.

Suzy winked at Shelly and said, "It is indeed a special song that I think is sung by many. Isn't that great?!"

"Let's go see," said Tarie. And they all walked over to watch and listen to The Segments and no one was surprised when they saw Curiosity on stage singing with The Segments as Curiosity very much loved music. 228

86

The Segments (nicknamed the 5 O's) are a breakout sister singing/ dancing act that started at a small club called The Juicer. At The Juicer they became aware of **PressThisButton** from The Juicer's owner - Juicy Lucy (a slice of watermelon with the cutest heart shaped glasses pictured below far left) who first discovered them. **PressThisButton** is a way to access answers to many questions, the Segments realized, and it was their red dancing boots that granted access to this awesome tool.

So one day they asked "Will we become big stars?" **PressThisButton** answered *Go deeper into your feelings and experience them now.* They thought about this answer and experienced a feeling from a way long time ago, or maybe it was just a little time ago, or maybe it was in the future, but the feeling was so strong and important to them that they took notice. The feeling was timeless! They caught that timeless feeling and remembered that it was associated with a song that they had always sang together. They knew and felt that the song was very important to them and sang that song for an audition at the exclusive, popular, invitation only nightclub The Punch Bowl. Overnight that very song "Highest Good" became a smash hit and they became a universal phenomenon. With **PressThisButton** they also became aware of a unique superpower. When they want to travel through time or space, they (the segments) join together and form a whole orange and in a 'blink' are transported anywhere they want to go - to the Miso Mice super yacht, the Zodiac Girls' star ports or anywhere else. Once they arrive at their destination they automatically separate back to individual slices.

Their back-up singers have been with them since they started at The Juicer. Juicy Lucy (The Juicer owner far left) Doley -the dancing pineapple; Coco - a crazy coconut from Jamacia, Aloha (the smiling pineapple from Hawaii), the cherry twins: Sweetie and Tarta and Prosperity the Fig.

102, 103, 104, 105

And yes, you may have figured out - The Segment's hit song is indeed the same as the Miso Mice special song. How cool is that?   The lyrics to "Highest Good" are below.

Open heart, open mind, for highest good,
for always and in all ways.
Lets all go with the flow and live for the moment…
Open heart, open mind…
Let's breath in and out and know that we will be happy with
open heart, open mind…
We're on a journey of learning and experiences
that make us whole…
open heart, open mind
for the highest good…for always and in all ways….
in all ways, for always…and always.

Adventure 7: Breakfast on the Mezzanine

106, 107

The morning after the Quantum Entanglement party, Cappy, Gemi, Tara, Le, and Can-Can had gotten up early to create an amazing buffet breakfast of almost unlimited choices, most of them including some form of cheese, as they knew that for their guests and themselves, cheese was very gouda and the Miso Mice were their soul swissters! 108

If you love cheese puns, ha, ha, ha - here are a couple more: in queso emergency; sorry you're feeling bleu. He's a real munster. I'll brie back. Nacho cheese – mine!

There were chefs manning stations for made-to-order omelets, waffles, French toast, blintzes and pancakes, with multiple cheeses available for stuffing and/or topping. There were quesadillas with extra cheese, cheesy bacon and sausage, cheese grits, a double cheese board, several types of cheese fondues and their universe famous donuts including their cheesecake filled one, in honor of their guests. But there were other choices on the buffet too including cereals, fruits and croissants as Ari had finally made it to the party last night, stayed overnight, and she adored a fresh from the oven croissant with sweet butter and strawberry jam. Knowing that sprite Kaame loved the Polish pastry kolachki, Can-Can had been busy baking them in all kinds of flavors since they woke up. Of course Sandman had his favorite tuna tartare but Freddie was no longer at the Star Port having won the "Way Too Many Cats" game tournament and decided to go casino surfing with the group of Pleiadian cats who came in second.

The buffet was set-up on the mezzanine and with the light of millions of sun stars shining brightly now, everyone was able to again see the City on the Edge of Forever, this time with it's labyrinth of happenings – things

zooming this way and that, up and down, sideways, appearing and disappearing. Everyone who visited the mezzanine always said that you could see things from a higher perspective here, and new alternatives to the "same old, same old" seemed to present themselves. It was a spectacular and mesmerizing view and as everyone gathered, Kaame stood and stared at the city, again feeling as if she had seen it before but she couldn't quite focus on the feeling. 109

"Wow this is an amazing buffet," remarked Suzy as she perused the incredible assortment of delicious looking food. "There's something here for everyone including Sandman and Freddie. What gracious hostesses you Zodiac Girls are! Did Freddie really jump on a transporter with the Pleiadians and go to Vegas last night?" she asked as she reached down to pet Sandman who was enjoying his breakfast.

"No. One of the catfishes that was in the tournament, Gumbo, needed a ride back to the Lobst-A-Lantis Casino and Freddie said that he and Tappy Greenshoes would be happy to take her as one casino is as good as another. If you ask me, Freddie and Tappy seemed pretty entangled last night," quipped Curiosity as she walked around the tables. "I think the Pleiadian cats went with them too but I'm not sure. Hmmm.... I love buffets! You have choices and can pick whatever and how much you want."

"That's like the 2 step process, choose'ndo that Tarie was explaining to us before the Quantum Entanglement party," said Polly

"Yes," laughed Shelly. "I never thought of a buffet that way, but that's exactly it! You go to the buffet, choose what you want and then 'do', put as much of it as you want on your plate – choose'ndo!" she finished as she too was looking over the buffet and surreptitiously snitched a piece of port salut, her current favorite cheese from the cheese board. As she munched on the cheese Shelly thought that's maybe exactly what everyone does. The Universe gives you an unlimited buffet of choices and you pick what you want. Wow! That's a very interesting idea she thought.

"That was a great party last night," Kat shared as she walked along the buffet tables and abruptly stopped. "I can't believe it! You made the universe famous Zodiac Girls' donuts! You are the best!" she exclaimed as she ran up to Tara and gave her a big hug.110

Tara hugged her back and laughed, "thank you so much but I didn't make them this time. Can-Can made them so you should thank her."

"Thank you so much! You know these are my favorite," said Kat as she turned to Can-Can and gave her a big hug. "Here's choose'ndo in action," she laughed as she picked up a long john donut that was stuffed with cream and covered with chocolate.

13

CHOOSE DONUT ➡ EAT DONUT

"Polly this is a credible process," she said in an authoritative voice and then ruined the authority by laughing. She took a big bite of the donut. "Yum! Not only credible but most delicious too. Now I understand why Polly loves being physical so much. You can't enjoy a donut like this if you are beyond-physical!" she laughed munching away and everyone joined Kat in her laughter and enjoyment of the donut.

"You're right Kat," said Tarie. "There are so many different things you can experience when you are physical, especially using the 5 senses of sight, sound, smell, taste and touch."

207

"Don't forget emotions and feelings!" added Aquie.

"Are those physical?" asked Polly.

"Ah, now that's a really good question," answered Tarie. "We can talk about that if you like. One idea is that emotions and feelings are a bridge between the beyond-physical and physical." [207]

"Well I know my sense of smell is physical as there's some delicious coffee coming," said Polly as she walked over to the beverage cart that Gemi was just wheeling out.

"Yes, yes, yes! Come and get it everyone! I have beverages right here," said Gemi as she wheeled the cart to the side of one of the buffet tables. "Let me see if I remember correctly. Polly, Suzy, and Kat you are the coffee fanatics and we have a new coffee maker where you choose and make your own, any way you want it. It was a gift from Sandman when he came to stay with Aquie as he knew how much she loved fresh-brewed coffee but always wanted to choose a different kind every time she had a cup. This coffee maker is great. The choices you can make are almost limitless. There are hundreds of flavors of coffee, cream, sugar, liquors and an infinite number of variations on all of them. All you have to do is press the buttons," Gemi said as she pointed to the coffee maker as Polly and Suzy came closer. [111]

"Oh that's funny Gemi – press the buttons! Did you mean ask your PressThisButton which coffee combo you should choose?" said Ari as everyone laughed.

"Ha ha ha very funny Ari. I guess either way – you choose'ndo," said Gemi.

"Well," said Polly, "to be credible there's really not an infinite number of variations, maybe lots, maybe even something like millions but not infinite."

"Well, I'll try one variation right now and that's plain black," laughed Suzy as she poured herself a cup and quipped. "That might be the first variation, or maybe the zero variation! Get it – zero variation – plain black coffee?"

"Yes Suzy we get it and there it is again, choose'ndo, the 2 step process and this time with coffee," said Shelly.

"I'm getting the feeling that it's not only with donuts or coffee or going into the sky, but with everything there's choose'ndo," said Polly. I'm going to ask PressThisButton if that's the process you use to get everything done as I was awake enough this morning to put it in my pocket!" said Polly as she took the button out. "I bet no one else thought of taking it!" *Coincidence is the solution in search of a problem.*

"Wow, I'm glad you did bring the button Polly as you've got your answer," laughed Shelly. "There you go. As Tarie said yesterday, PressThisButton always has the answer!"

"But what's the answer?" asked Polly. "I don't get it."

"Polly," said Curiosity very gently, "you had a problem, and it's no coincidence that a solution for it has been given to you bazillions of times between yesterday and today and that solution is - YES! If you want to get something done choose'ndo!!!!!!"

"Well I wouldn't say that it was a problem, more of a question," Polly defended.

"How many times did you have to ask the question Polly?" Suzy asked.

"I just wanted to be sure that it was a credible answer – that choose'ndo was credible and OK I got my answer, again, and again, and again. I now formally and with authority acknowledge and am aware that choose'ndo is a credible answer to the question on how to get things done," Polly said solemnly.

"I think it's also Universe Rule #1 – everything gets to choose," added Kaame as although she was still standing closer to the view she had turned toward the others who were by the buffet tables idle chattering. "I have no idea where I just got that from!" she exclaimed a bit surprised at herself for saying that as it seemed to just blurt out of her without her even thinking – a knowing without words she thought. 112

"At this point I would agree with you. I think there's credible evidence that it is indeed Universe Rule #1 – everything gets to choose, but then they have to follow through with the do to get it done," said Polly as by that time she had walked over to the buffet table and was choosing what she wanted to eat for breakfast. "It does take two steps."

"Kaame, don't you want something to eat?" asked Tarie as she quietly walked over to her and handed her a rainbow sprite juice. "Your favorite – right?"

"Oh yes, that's my favorite. Thanks so much for remembering," said Kaame and as an afterthought added, "or did you just know? You seem to 'just know' lots of things, kind of like Suzy."

"You too 'just know' lots of things. I think you're on the edge of what we Zodiac Girls describe as riding the stream of intuition, coincidences, synchronicity and direct knowing; flowing with what resonates with you – what feels right. Or in simpler terms, 'going with the flow'," explained Tarie. "What do you think about the City on The Edge of Forever?" asked Tara as she came up to Kaame and Tarie.

"For some reason I feel like I've been there," said Kaame.

"Oh – maybe that's where we met you," Tara said to Kaame and then turned to the group who had made their selections from the buffet table and were now sitting down eating. "Hey everyone," said Tara to get their attention as she pointed to the city they could see in the view from the mezzanine level. "Did you all know that the houses in the city are very

113

unique? They have timeless views where you can look out into infinity and see forever. The windows in the houses are gateways where as you look out, you can create pictures of your future self and your experiences, as many as you like. It's like creating a video game of yourself. You choose the characters and the action. It's really kind of cool."

"Use this house in timelessness to look out into infinity as the views from this house are from forever," Kaame said in a whisper while having the same feeling that she just knew something from experience, she had experienced it before but it wasn't quite taking shape.

"Ahh, so maybe you have been in the City on the Edge of Forever before Kamme," surmised Tarie with a gentle knowing look. "I think maybe that's indeed where we met you, at least one time before, as you seem to know things about the city. But enough of that now, let's go choose'ndo the buffet table before the Miso Mice eat all of the cheese! Although I know your favorite are the Polish kolachki and Can-Can baked a huge assortment of them for you," said Tarie as she guided Kaame toward the buffet table.

"I would love to see those houses," said Shelly munching on a triple Muenster, Gouda, Cheddar cheese omelet with double extra Brie melted on top and a side serving of parmesan encrusted bacon on toast topped with melted mozzarella cheese. Shelly really did love cheese!

"I'm not sure if I find that credible – windows on houses that are gateways where you can picture your future selves and they are unlimited?" asked Polly taking a bite of one of the freshly baked croissants that she had topped with sweet butter and homemade blueberry jam. "This is delicious!"

"It's choose'ndo coupled with imagination," responded Curiosity who had chosen a vegetarian omelet topped with a bit of cheddar cheese and kielbasa on the side.

"And once you choose'ndo as **PressThisButton** answered, *The Universe will arrange the string of events to get this done in the shortest time possible."* said Kaame as she, Tarie and Tara made their way to the buffet table to choose'ndo.

Adventure 8: The Zodiac Girls Jewelry

As breakfast wound down and no one could eat another bite, not even another donut for Kat or piece of cheese for Shelly, the Miso Mice and Kaame offered to help clean-up but the Zodiac Girls wouldn't hear of it. "Thank you so much for the offer," said Can-Can but we'll take care of everything. We just recently installed the new Techno-Cleano that Freddie suggested as he had seen one on Animal Planet and all we have to do is put away any food we want, close the area to be cleaned, and somehow it magically cleans itself!"

"What??? Are you serious? I don't know about that. Is it credible?" asked Polly. "I would like to see how that's done."

"I've actually thought about something like that for a long time – just close the door and the area gets cleaned," said Suzy. "In fact I think I've got some information at CAT on how it works."

"Wait, I thought CAT was the Center for Awareness Techniques. Why would you have information about a cleaning thing at CAT?" asked Shelly.

"Shelly, haven't you figured out yet that everything has to do with awareness?" asked Curiosity a bit impatiently. "The techniques are just suggestions, like using your imagination. Just be aware, listen to yourself, and you can get anything done. Or like we said ad nauseam during breakfast, choose'ndo," said Curiosity. 114

"I'm not sure how it's done, as the fine print says, 'once you close the area, do not enter under any circumstances until the time is up or ELSE' so we've never looked in to see how it's done but when the time is up, everything is put away in spic-n-span shape!" said Can-Can. "We haven't lost any dishes, cups or silverware yet and nothing's been broken. I think it's got something to do with the Quantum Entanglement stuff but I'm not an expert on that in the least. I choose to spend my time on other things," said Can-Can, "but I'll let Tarie know you asked and maybe she can help you. She just took the rest of the fruit back to the kitchen. Everyone just grab a re-fill on a beverage if you like, and go relax and we'll join you in a sec," said Can-Can as she placed what was left of the omelet station selections on a tray and took them back to refrigerate in the kitchen.

Suzy, Polly and Kat selected new coffees, Curiosity made another cup of her 100% organic sustainably farmed non-GMO green tea with a splash of turmeric, and Shelly still did sneak a couple of pieces of Stilton and Cheshire cheeses on a napkin. Suzy said, "To answer your question about having info on the Techno-Cleano in CAT, I have info on all kinds of things and like Curiosity said, everything has to do with awareness. The more you're aware, the more you can choose'ndo – experience what you want as opposed to what just happens to you. You can choose'ndo from the inside out instead of the outside in."

"Do you also have info on why the Zodiac Girls make jewelry? I was wondering about that," asked Kaame as they all settled themselves on the couches closer to the views of the City on the Edge of Forever. 115

"I know that they use sea glass, ocean stones and shells and other things too to make jewelry – star dust, rainbows, light beams, those kind of things too," said Kat as she sipped her coffee and was wondering if she should go to the kitchen and grab another donut before Can-Can put them away. "Hmmm, maybe I can design some outfits using those kinds of things. Maybe some dancing dresses for when we sing our song? Or maybe our own Oscar Awards dresses?" 116

"I think they also use time crystals," said Suzy, "and I would love to see some of those pieces of jewelry. I'll have to talk to the Zodiac Girls about time crystals as I've got a presentation on them and could add more information if they know something more or different than I have."

117

"Totally agree with you Suzy! Time crystals most likely would be able to help you travel through time," concluded Curiosity.

"Or just look really beautiful on any outfit as crystals shine and glitter," mused Kat.

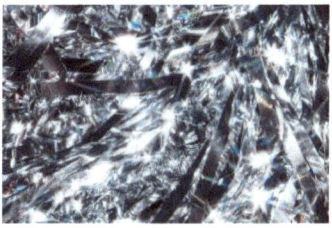

"I'm still trying to figure out the details about the time crystals Curiosity, but I know that they indeed would help you travel through time. Anyhow, why in the world would they be called time crystals if they didn't? Hmmmm...... Maybe they're a source of power or energy?" queried Suzy. "Maybe the Zodiac Girls know the details. And yes of course Kat, they are beautiful and would look great on any outfit." 118

"Let's ask PressThisButton why the Zodiac Girls make jewelry," said Polly changing the subject to answer Kaame's question as she pulled the button out of her pocket. *Focus on what you wish to become. Focus on your abilities. You have what you need for growth. The Universe will provide the ways and the means*. I love PressThisButton! That makes sense! The Zodiac Girls make jewelry because they are focusing on their abilities. Their jewelry is beautiful and known throughout the whole Universe. The Universe and we too are providing the things they need to make the jewelry and they are growing because of it – WOW!! I think I'm becoming more and more aware of things as these answers are really starting to make sense for me."

"Talking about jewelry," said Tarie as she came back to the group, "these are for each of you. These pieces of jewelry will help you find The Answer Book."

As Tarie handed a piece of jewelry to each of the Miso Mice, they all began to look more and more at their pieces in awe as they each had a feeling, a memory, that they recognized these pieces from another time. Where did they see them? Were these pieces of jewelry actually made from time crystals and were they appearing and disappearing through time?

  "Oh my!" exclaimed Curiosity. "This necklace is the tree of life that shows how I see my position when I choose physical things and the "vintage truck" has most definitely been "haunting" me at the next episode of my travels. I've been thinking that maybe I should build this truck." [119, 120]

"Do you know how to build a truck?" asked Kaame.

"Oh with my imagination, most definitely!" replied Curiosity.

"This chocolate diamond mama bear was a Christmas gift from some time ago," said Suzy. "I know it has matching earrings."

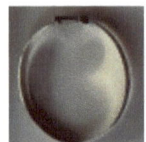 "And this circular bracelet has a cool print on the 2 silver bands. It was from Ireland and I never took it off; it was always with me," said Kat.

"My tiara is related to something else – some other type of crown or tiara I have," remembered Shelly.[121]

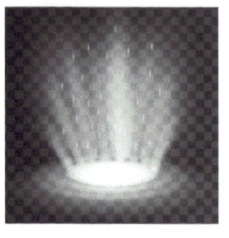

"And I was moving houses and this necklace was the only piece of jewelry that I had not packed," said Polly.

"I wonder why we feel that we all know these pieces?" asked Suzy. "Could these pieces be made out of time crystals?" Suzy continued to ponder as she turned her piece of jewelry over and then exclaimed, "Look on the back of your jewelry everyone! It's PressThisButton! I just knew we had these before! These were our own PressThisButton!"

"Wow!" exclaimed Shelly, "We had our own PressThisButton! That's why these pieces all feel so familiar. We've seen them before."

"Tarie said that these pieces of jewelry would help us find *The Answer Book*," reminded Polly. "We must ask PressThisButton how the jewelry will help. But who should ask? As we all have our own PressThisButton?"

"It doesn't matter," said Curiosity, "Remember Quantum Entanglement? Everything is entangled with everything else so no matter who asks, we'll get the answer we need. *Vary your way of thinking. Look for new ways, new styles, new colors. Stay in the now and refocus your thinking to a new, higher level.*"

"I'm still puzzled about the jewelry pieces but I think the answer means that we've seen this jewelry before, but now we have to think about it in a different, new, higher level way, not just as jewelry. To find *The Answer Book* we have to vary our way of thinking…..but how do we do that? Hmmmm…..let's ask PressThisButton *Understanding comes from intuition, experience and knowing. Vary your thinking and go directly to knowing*. The answer keeps coming back to vary our way of thinking…..intuition and experience…..direct knowing…..hmmm….what should we think differently? Maybe this all has to do with time crystals. Where would you be if you were *The Answer Book*? Kaame, any ideas?" asked Suzy as she looked directly at Kaame.

122

Kaame was startled that she was singled out by Suzy and said, "I'm not sure. Something about the intuition, experience and direct knowing is ringing a bell with me but I can't quite place it. They're feelings without words."

"That's exactly it! These jewelry pieces are part of the answer," interrupted Curiosity. "We know these pieces and have special awesome feelings, without words, about them. That's the intuition and knowing. Feelings come from inside ourselves. We just have to look at finding *The Answer Book* in a different way – go from the inside out! Let's use our imagination! Maybe the time crystal parts of the jewelry have us thinking inside out!"

"I'm thinking about the context for inside-out and outside-in credible comfort zones," Polly said as she analyzed the situation. "We're more comfortable with what we know, but like Curiosity says, other perspectives exist, and

seeing things from another's point of view definitely offers another perspective. And I suppose, seeing things from the inside out would definitely be another perspective. That's 6 and 9!"[123]

"Or my 'be the IQQker of the thinker'," added Curiosity. "Just stand behind yourself and see through yourself and what do you see?"

"Curiosity, I'm not sure if that works for me," said Shelly becoming frustrated at all of this information with no really concrete instructions. [124]

"Remember Tarie said that for some it's really simple and obvious and for others not so much so. Remember when we got the answer to the question: what is choose'ndo? *Take some deep breaths, relax, and flow with your higher energy.* For Curiosity the answer meant use your imagination. For Polly it meant use meditation, and for you it was specific instructions. It's different for everyone but begins inside you – your intuition, experience and direct knowing – those are all inside out things," said Kat.

"And what's the adventure we're on?" asked Suzy. *"To find The Answer Book – to realize what is within your chosen created self which creates your chosen future reality.* And it looks like we're figuring out pretty quickly that it starts from inside and that there are many unique ways as to how the realization or awareness happens."

"I think I'm getting it," responded Shelly slowly. "We all have special pieces of jewelry to help us figure this out and I wonder if Kaame has a special piece of jewelry? Kaame, ask your PressThisButton "

"OK, that sounds good. I would love to have a special piece of jewelry too," said Kaame. "I think my own special piece of jewelry would help me catch these timeless feelings that have been floating around my head. *Think of the patterns of the waves on the ocean – always moving. Your new thinking, direct knowing, will move like the waves on the ocean, fluid and mobile."*

125

"It seems to be the same answer in a different way," said Kat. "We have to vary our way of thinking, open our mind to new patterns and go to direct knowing and that means you too Kaame."

"I know one way we can do that – through timewalking!" suggested Suzy.

"And now that we have our jewelry that may have time crystals in it, timewalking will be easy!" added Kat.

"Most excellent – yes – let's all do it but first let's all sing our special song," exclaimed Shelly, "as I think timewalking will take all of us on a new adventure!"

"Should I get all of us new outfits for this song?" asked Kat.

"I don't think there's time as it seems that we're really going with the flow here," replied Suzy, "we'll just have to sing with what we're wearing now. Kaame, you too. You know our song now too."

Open heart, open mind, for highest good, for always and in all ways

232, 233

"If we're going timewalking I'm going back to the sailing ship to get my comfy shoes. Does anyone want anything else?" asked Polly.

"Polly, you know that timewalking doesn't necessarily mean actually walking," said Curiosity.

"That's OK, I wanted to change into those shoes after breakfast anyhow. I'll be back in a minute," said Polly.

Adventure 9: Timewalkers

126, 127

Polly actually returned in more like 5 minutes and heard Suzy say, "Kaame, choose a place to timewalk where your special jewelry will be revealed."

"A jewelry store would be the obvious place," said Polly as she re-joined the group.

"I think much better jewelry can be found on a beach," replied Shelly.

"I think the stars are the best place to find jewelry," suggested Can-Can.

"I don't think you need to go anywhere – just use your imagination," said Curiosity.

"Remember that the answers to our questions have been to vary our way of thinking, use intuition, experience, and direct knowing. Kaame, keeping that in mind, you choose – where would you like to go?" asked Suzy again.

Kaame replied, "I'm going to ask PressThisButton where I should go timewalking to find my special piece of jewelry. *Vary your way of thinking. Look for new ways, new styles, new colors. Stay in the now and refocus your thinking to a new, higher level.*

"Oh no! Here it is again! The Universe is hitting us over the head and we're just not getting something!" exclaimed Shelly exasperated.

"I can't believe it," said Polly. "That's the same answer that we got when we asked how the jewelry can help us find *The Answer Book*! WOW - We definitely have to think differently! We've gotten that same answer 3 times now. That's no coincidence – the Universe is definitely trying to tell us something."

"I told you, use your imagination!" said Curiosity, "With your imagination you can think any way you want – you get to choose everything!"

"Doesn't timewalking use imagination?" asked Polly. "Let's go somewhere where we can get our imagination going."

"You don't have to go anywhere" said Curiosity. "Just think. If you want, be the IQQker of the thinker and there are lots of ways to do that! You can  imagine standing behind yourself and as you think, look into and through yourself. Or you can do it by listening, and experiencing your favorite song – be the music! Just go inside yourself, look out and think non-linear! Think in a zig-zag way, ping pong around in your head. It's your choice how you do it. Remember what the book in the bottle on the beach said, 'Just do it"! 128

"Kaame, you can use any of Curiosity's suggestions or also what PressThisButton answered *Vary your way of thinking. Look for new ways, new styles, new colors. Stay in the now and refocus your thinking to a new, higher level.*

Kaame closed her eyes and Suzy asked, "Kaame what are you thinking?"

"I'm not 'thinking' anything. I'm clearing my mind of all thoughts and just floating. I'm picturing the City on the Edge of Forever. I have a house there. I'm in my house, opening the big picture window and see the timeless view that looks out into infinity. I can see forever! I'm picturing my future self with my jewelry and I'm holding

my necklace!" said Kaame excitedly as she touched her necklace. "My special piece of jewelry is my necklace which is my PressThisButton!" she said in awe as she opened her eyes. "I just know it! I know it!"

"Yes of course it is as you've had it with you all the time. That's what our special pieces of jewelry are – our own timeless PressThisButtons. They're a treasure that we've had all along that will help us answer any question that we have. 50, 109

Wow that seems pretty easy," said Shelly in awe, "and Kaame didn't even have special instructions or anything!"

"It's different for everyone - awareness, realization, resonance; and only happens when you're ready," said Cappy. "Sometimes you need a little Quantum Entanglement, or to picture your future self from a window in a house in the City on the Edge of Forever to vary your way of thinking to a new higher level of intuition and direct knowing to find some treasure!"

Suzy had been quiet for a while, thinking about everyone's chatter. Did Cappy just say treasure? Hmmmm….another coincidence? No coincidences. The Miso Mice PressThisButton floated out of a treasure chest and we have that treasure chest on our sailing ship…..hmmm…..is there more treasure in there?

"Suzy, now that we all have our special pieces of jewelry let's keep looking for *The Answer Book*. I'm going to ask PressThisButton what we should do next to find *The Answer Book*. *View your thoughts as colors. Focus on the feelings of those thoughts, of your experience as you feel, on your higher self. Use these feelings to increase your vibrations.*129

Suzy was concentrating on her piece of jewelry as she thought about this answer and treasure. Focus on: thoughts as colors, feelings of thoughts, experience as you feel, your higher self? Use feelings to increase your vibrations? Suzy suddenly had an inspiration and said, "I need to ask PressThisButton where I should go timewalking *Your thoughts intersect other's thoughts and influence each other. Thoughts with deep feelings strongly influence others. You exist in both a timeless and timed framework. Focus on limited time and linear thought. Focus with your higher self.*

With that answer, everyone watched as Suzy closed her eyes, sang the Miso Mice special song:

Open heart, open mind, for highest good, for always and in all ways,

and did exactly as PressThisButton suggested. She was so focused on her higher self and increasing her vibrations that she didn't even ask the rest of the Miso Mice and Kaame to sing with her! Suzy was definitely going with the flow now.

130

Adventure 10: Tem-E-Laks

After a bit of time, or maybe it was not so much a bit but a longer time, Suzy opened her eyes and said, "I have to go back to our sailing ship now. I was timewalking to the treasure chest that we found and when I opened it there were 5 boxes in it that I have to give to each of you. Wait here, I'll get what I need," yelled Suzy as she ran back to their sailing ship, opened the treasure chest and 5 boxes magically floated out. Suzy gathered the boxes and returned back to everyone. "Just like I saw while I timewalked. They have each of our names on them. Here, everyone take theirs," said Suzy as she handed out the boxes.

TEMporary
Enhanced
Light
Amplified
Knowledge

Polly opened her box and said, "These are words. What could they mean?"

"My box contains a time tunnel," said Curiosity as she opened it. "I don't think I can take it out as when I put my hand in, my hand disappears. This is really cool!" 131

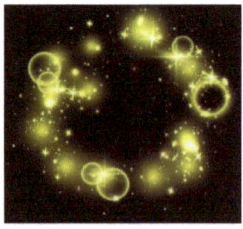

"Oh my!" exclaimed Shelly, "My box has a beautiful sparkly circle star crown!" As Shelly took out the tiara, the sparkles shot out golden rays of ethereal lights that seemed to go on forever and Shelly just knew that this tiara had something to do with her tiara piece of jewelry. This was no coincidence! 132

"Mine looks like a tiara too," said Kat as she opened her box. 133

Inside Suzy's box was a wreath of beautiful laurel leaves. "Look at the box, there's information on it," said Suzy as she turned the box over. "Wow, when I went timewalking I was thinking about the answers we had gotten from **PressThisButton** about looking at things in new ways, varying our thinking, going to direct knowing and intersecting thoughts and I did. These are tools from the Universe! 134

From: The Universe
To: Suzy Butterfly
Contents: 1 Tem-E-Lak Energy Tool

Choose How to Use

"Is that label on each of our boxes," asked Polly as she turned her box over and indeed it was the same label but the "to" person was Polly Hedron. Each of the Miso Mice were checking their boxes and they each had the same label with their own names in the "to" section. "But why did you get the boxes and not each of us? And what is a Tem-E-Lak Energy Tool?"

"I was the one who went timewalking and when I opened the treasure chest the 5 boxes floated out. I was supposed to find them and give them to you," said Suzy.

What's this "choose how to use?" asked Shelly. "You think they would give you instructions!" she added exasperated again at the lack of specific instructions on how to use the Tem-E-Lak energy tools. Shelly really liked it better when she had instructions that told her in a step by step fashion how to choose'ndo.

"They did give you instructions," said Curiosity. "You choose how to use – those are the instructions! You get to choose! I do not understand at all why this is so difficult for everyone!" 135

"Wait one minute! Shelly, back when Kaame figured out her special jewelry, what was it you said about treasure?"

"Ummm….let me think," replied Shelly. "I don't remember."

"She said, 'They're a treasure that we've had all along that will help us answer any question that we have,' said Kaame. "And when we were on the beach Curiosity said that the Miso Mice PressThisButton floated out from a magical treasure chest."

"And these Tem-E-Laks are energy tools that were in the treasure chest," thought Suzy as she zoomed along the stream of direct knowing in her mind. 136

"We've got to go back to the treasure chest!" shouted Suzy and Kaame in unison as they looked at each other as awareness dawned on them. They both just knew that another clue to where *The Answer* Book was in the treasure chest.

"Quick, everyone, back to our sailing ship," said Suzy as she and Kaame took off running to the ship while all of the other Miso Mice looked at each other and then jumped up to follow. 137

138

Adventure 11: The Treasure Chest

Suzy was the first to arrive at the sailing ship and bounded down the steps to the cargo hold where they had stored the  treasure chest. Kaame was right behind her and the other Miso Mice arrived only a couple of seconds later. "Where's the treasure chest?" Suzy asked as she looked all over the cargo hold that was jam packed with the Miso Mice's must have travel items, accoutrements, paraphernalia, Shelly's entire seashell collection, and a majority of Kat's adventure/sailing wardrobe. "I was just down here and it was right here." 139

 "Yes – that's where I saw it too. When I came back to the ship to get my slippers it was right here," said Polly motioning to the right side of the stairs where they had always stored the treasure chest. "You all know we keep it right here as everyone wanted easy access to PressThisButton and we all agreed that this was the best place. Remember? We talked about it when we first set sail," Polly said defensively. 140

"Why did you come down here to get your slippers?" asked Shelly.

"I didn't come down for my slippers. Since we realized that the pieces of jewelry the Zodiac Girls gave us were our own PressThisButton I thought it would make sense to put the one that floated out of the treasure chest back so we wouldn't lose it," explained Polly.

"Oh that makes sense," acknowledged Curiosity. "Suzy, are you sure it was here next to the stairs? Did someone put it someplace else?" asked Curiosity as she looked at the other Miso Mice and Kaame.

"I don't know who could have done that. Both Suzy and I were down here a little bit ago and you know how I like to be credible, so it really was just a little bit ago," emphasized Polly, "and all of you were still on the mezzanine."

"What could have happened to it?" asked Kat as everyone began looking around the cargo hold, moving items this way and that to see if the treasure chest was anywhere to be found.

"You know, I need my sand dollar collection anyhow as I wanted to compare the one Curiosity found on the beach with my other ones so maybe it's good that we're down here. Did anyone see the collection?" asked Shelly.

"Ha ha – you know – no coincidences, only the Universe trying to tell us something," reminded Curiosity, "and here you go Shelly," said Curiosity as she handed Shelly the sand dollar collection and went back to the boxes she was looking at. "So cool! Here's my stuff on organic non-GMO gardening!" she exclaimed as she peeked into the box below the sand dollar collection.

"We can choose'ndo to do this on board our ship," she thought out loud as she began flipping through the books and magazines. "You know organic is much healthier." 141

Kat who had been looking at the area around the stairs, reached down and picked up a white object. "What's this?" she asked as everyone stopped what they were doing and came over to Kat to see what she had found.

"That looks like the sand dollar that Curiosity found on the beach," answered Shelly. "But I have that one in my shell box upstairs as I was going to compare it to these sand dollars," she explained as she motioned to the box she was holding, "as both Curiosity and I thought it was just too perfect, and looking at this one," she continued as she took the sand dollar from Kat, "this one seems to be just a bit too perfect too." Shelly handed the sand dollar to Curiosity, "what do you think Curiosity?"

"Yes indeed. These are the work of Lobsta. No one ever listens to me! I told you at the beach that Lobsta knows something about *The Answer Book* and now he's stolen our treasure chest! I just know it! This is proof! He or one of his minions was here!" said Curiosity as she stamped her foot. "I should have taken care of him when I could have with the 6 and 9 incident!" 226

"Curiosity, seriously, how would you have taken care of him?" asked Suzy skeptically. "We were all there and you did your best to explain to him that everyone chooses to see things as they want, and just because he and you saw things differently didn't mean that either one was right or wrong – just different."

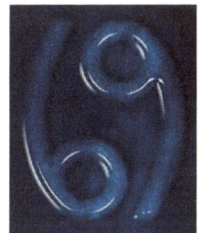

"And I even tried to help explain, as you know, that's one of my favorite sayings, 'you see a 6 but I see an upside 9'. Curiosity, you did your best and there was nothing else to do, as obviously, at that time, Lobsta was not aware that as the saying goes, 'he could agree to disagree' with you and still be friends," interrupted Polly. 37

"Well we can't do anything about that now. We've got to take this sand dollar upstairs and compare it to the other sand dollar and the ones in this box," said Shelly as she motioned for everyone to move to the stairs.

They all went up as quickly as possible and piled into Shelly's room that of course was decorated curtesy of Kat, in a beautiful beach motif. Shelly brought out the sand dollar from the beach and placed it on the bed with the one Kat had found where the treasure chest should have been, and opened the box containing her collection. Everyone began investigating

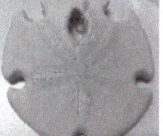
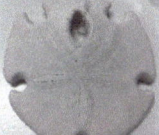

the sand dollars looking for differences. "There's no question about it. These 2 are different from the ones in the collection. The ones from my collection have holes in different places than these 2. The differences are very subtle. You have to give credit to Lobsta. These counterfeit sand dollars are very good," observed Shelly.

"I can say with 100% credibility that these 2 sand dollars are different than Shelly's and it seems to me, I think these are made out of some type of lucite-sand composite, but to be sure we'd have to do a lab analysis," concluded Polly as she held one of each to more closely inspect them. "I don't think these 2 sand dollars are made by nature."

"I told you! It's all Lobsta's doing!" said Curiosity exasperated.

"OK, I give you that these 2 sand dollars may be fake sand dollars, but how can you be sure that these fake sand dollars are from Lobsta?" asked Kat.

"Remember the whole 6 and 9 thing, when we were all at Clams Casino playing roulette? He picked his favorite number 6 and I was sitting on the other side of the roulette wheel and I said it was a 9, because of course it was upside-down for me. He started yelling that it was his lucky number, 6, and I kept razzing him that it was a 9 and even pointed to the 9 on my side of the wheel. He got so mad that he took off in a huff and left a couple of his sand dollars on the table and I noticed that they seemed weird somehow, but of course Shelly's the expert on sea shells and such. The sand dollars that Lobsta left just seemed too perfect. There is no coincidence, only the Universe telling you things and the Universe is telling me that these are Lobsta's counterfeited sand dollars and that he now has our treasure chest," explained Curiosity.[142]

"Well I guess that this really can't be a coincidence as the probability of these sand dollars and Lobsta's at Clams Casino being the same are way too high. I agree with Curiosity in that Lobsta is a very credible suspect," deduced Polly.

"OK, if everyone is in agreement, we'll drop Sandman off at the Rainbow Bridge and then proceed on to Lobsta's casino," finalized Suzy. "Let's go tell the Zodiac Girls and Sandman."

Meanwhile, back in Lobsta's office....

"Here you go boss," said Big Tuna as he knocked on Lobsta's door, waited for him to say "come in", and then walked in with Man O. Warren and Indigo Blue and a sea dragon that had a treasure chest tied to the top of it. "We'ves gots it!" he said victoriously. [143, 204]

"Oh ho! Yes – the treasure chest!" exclaimed Lobsta clicking his claws and jumping up from his desk chair as he spied the treasure chest. "Bring it right over here boys. Just put it on this table." Lobsta motioned to the coffee table in front of the couch. "Let's see what treasure they've been hiding," he said rubbing his claws and chortling. Squidella who had been

PRESS THIS BUTTON

sitting in front of Lobsta's desk click-clacked her way over to the treasure chest. Lobsta opened the chest and things started to float out: a button, a kaleidoscope, a magnifying glass, a sun catcher, an airplane, cutlery, an artist's palette, pencil, and lots of crystal pieces of all kinds of shapes, sizes and colors. "What? This is junk! This isn't treasure! Where's the book with the treasure maps? You guys got the wrong chest!" Lobsta angrily yelled at everyone while Squidella began to catch the things that were floating around and placing them on the table. [229]

144, 145, 146, 147, 148, 149

"Boss, these may be jewels," said Big Tuna as he caught a couple of the pieces of crystal and showed them to Lobsta.

"Big Tuna, those are made of glass and even if they were jewels there's not enough of them to be any big treasure. I tell you, do I have to do everything myself?" Lobsta asked as he pointed to Indigo Blue and Man O. Warren.

"Boss, this was the only treasure chest on that ship! We looked all over and the rest was just the Miso Mice stuff. There was no other treasure chest boss, we're sure. We promise! Cross our hearts and hope to die," said Man O. Warren defensively.

"Lobsta, Man O. Warren and Indigo Blue are 2 of our best guys. If they say this was the only treasure chest, I believe them. Maybe there's a false bottom or sides where something else is hidden and these are just decoys," suggested Squidella as she looked into the treasure chest and started pulling at the bottom and sides to see if they would break away or open up. She then inspected the top and saw this:

From: The Universe
To: Those Who are Interested
Contents: Energy Tools

Choose How to Use

Choose'ndo

"Wait a minute. Look at the top. What is this?" asked Squidella as everyone came around her to peer at the top of the treasure chest.

Lobsta leaned over Squidella and read the words. "That's just some stupid stuff. Really? From the Universe? To those who are interested? Energy tools – a pencil, a magnifying glass? Choose how to use? You got to watch out for that Curiosity! Sometimes she's just one step ahead of us and I think she took the real treasure and put it somewhere else and put this junk in as a joke. I gotta give her credit! Her imagination is incredible!" said Lobsta in appreciation of a job well done. "She's got the real treasure. I just know it!"

PRESS
THIS
BUTTON

Big Tuna caught the button that was floating around and looked at it more closely. He read the front and back and then asked, "I wonder what this is?" and pressed the button.
The thoughts stored in your mind influence you and others. WHATT??!! "Boss, this button just answered my question," stammered Big Tuna holding the button in his palm out to Lobsta.

INSTRUCTIONS:
ASK A QUESTION
THEN
PRESS THIS BUTTON
Choose'ndo

"What?" asked Lobsta who had decided that there was no treasure in this chest and had gone back to sit at his desk. "What do you mean the button answered your question?"

"Boss, I caught this green button that was floatin' around, read the instructions, and then asked 'I wonder what this is?' and the button answered, "*The thoughts stored in your mind influence you and others.*" related Big Tuna as he walked over to Lobsta.

"If that was your question, that's no answer. Let me see that button," said Lobsta grabbing the button out of Big Tuna's hand. Lobsta was inspecting it as the others gathered around him. He read the instructions out loud.

"Well ask it a question," concluded Squidella.

"Here's the real question," said Lobsta, "where's the treasure? And then he pressed the button *Higher thought is not limited to old outdated ideas but how do you move beyond the old and onto new higher patterns and designs?* "That's an answer? How does that tell me where the treasure is?" asked Lobsta looking at everyone in disgust.

"Boss, you knows I'm not much of one of those thinker types, but I think this means that we's got to do something more newer," speculated Big Tuna.

"Big Tuna is totally right. Maybe we should re-think this whole idea about treasure being jewels," said Squidella. "Thinking in a higher way, treasure could be," Squidella looked around the room trying to give a good example of what she was thinking, "Gumbo!"

"Gumbo's not treasure," replied Lobsta petting her. "She's my most favorite thing ever. I would do anything for her."

"Isn't that a treasure Lobsta? Something that you value above all else?" asked Squidella.

"Yah," said Big Tuna. "My answer was that thinking in your head affects you and others. Maybe we gots to think different. Boss, yous is always telling me to let yous choose to let me in when I knock on the door. Isn't that the thing? Yous choose what you want? Can't you choose to think that Gumbo is a treasure even if she ain't jewels? That's different thinking and it affects you and Gumbo." Lobsta looked at Big Tuna and thought that maybe he was losing his mind as what Big Tuna just said actually made sense to Lobsta. Maybe Gumbo was treasure.

"Let's ask the button again," said Squidella as she took the button from Lobsta. "Do you get to choose what you want? *Put yourself inside of your favorite picture and see it from this new perspective. Hear the sounds, feel the emotions and experience it from inside out.* "Wow!" exclaimed Squidella. "It looks like the answer is a resounding yes!"

"How is that a yes?" asked Lobsta skeptically but he was intrigued by the ideas that you got to choose, and that treasure didn't have to be jewels or money. Maybe treasure was something more.

"The button told us to look at things in a new perspective, from the inside out. We should look at treasure from a new perspective and maybe other things too. We do get to choose what we want," answered Squidella. "I'm not sure about all the other stuff, but I think this button thing may be valuable. We should keep this."

"OK, OK, I don't care – keep what you want. I think it's all pretty much junk," said Lobsta as he went back to his old thinking and dismissed the whole idea of new thinking, choosing, and treasure being something more than jewels or money. That can't be - can it? He didn't think like that before, why now? Lobsta was getting quite confused. He watched as Squidella gathered up all of the things that had floated out of the treasure chest including **PressThisButton**, put them back inside and closed the chest. "Squidella, I think we're done for now. Everyone can leave," said Lobsta as he went back to his desk thinking about what Big Tuna and Squidella had said.

Is it really so simple? Take charge, choose what you want instead of just letting stuff happen to you? Treasure doesn't have to just be money? He really would do anything for Gumbo. Ya, he had to admit, Gumbo was a treasure for him. Well, he thought, there's one way to find out. He went to the treasure chest and took out **PressThisButton** and said out loud, "Do you really get to choose what you want?" *Choose your thoughts and believe in your intuition and dreams to become what you choose.* Lobsta was totally gobsmacked and so startled by the answer that he dropped the button back into the treasure chest, closed the lid, and backed away. Maybe this was like Big Tuna said about the knocking, and Lobsta choosing whether to let Big Tuna come in or not. Lobsta was becoming aware of this new thinking - that there was lots more that he could choose - maybe everything, he wondered? Maybe this new thinking wasn't so bad. Maybe this new thinking was actually really good? 150

151

Adventures of the Miso Mice continue in Misos on a Mission

185

Appendix: Picture Attributes

Numbers on the bottom of pictures or at the end of a section correspond to their attributes located in this appendix.

1. <a href="https://www.freepik.com/vectors/melody">Melody vector created by freepik - www.freepik.com</a>
2. <a href="https://www.freepik.com/vectors/mice">Mice vector created by nizovatina - www.freepik.com</a>
14. <a href="https://www.freepik.com/vectors/mice >Mice vector created by freepik - www.freepik.com</a>
37. <a href="https://www.freepik.com/photos/galaxy-stars">Galaxy stars photo created by Allexxandar - www.freepik.com</a>
50. <a href="https://www.freepik.com/photos/necklace">Necklace photo created by wirestock - www.freepik.com</a>
83. <a href="https://www.freepik.com/vectors/valentines-day-poster">Valentines day poster vector created by freepik - www.freepik.com</a>
84. <a href="https://www.freepik.com/vectors/cute-cartoon">Cute cartoon vector created by jcomp - www.freepik.com </a>
85. <a href="https://www.freepik.com/vectors/astronaut-illustration">Astronaut illustration vector created by brgfx - www.freepik.com</a>
86. <a href="https://www.freepik.com/vectors/hand-drawing">Hand drawing vector created by coolvector - www.freepik.com</a>
87. <a href="https://www.freepik.com/vectors/meteor">Meteor vector created by macrovector - www.freepik.com</a>
88. <a href="https://www.freepik.com/vectors/set">Set vector created by pikisuperstar - www.freepik.com</a>
89. <a href="https://www.freepik.com/vectors/sugar-skull">Sugar skull vector created by upklyak - www.freepik.com</a>
90. <a href="https://www.freepik.com/vectors/emotions">Emotions vector created by user10320847 www.freepik.com</a>
91. <a href="https://www.freepik.com/vectors/happy-character">Happy character vector created by upklyak - www.freepik. com</a>
92. <a href="https://www.freepik.com/free-vector/cute-world-planet-cartoon-character_30979022.htm#page=40&query= cute &position=6&from_view=search">Image by brgfx</a> on Freepik
93. https://weird-giraffe-games.square.site/way-too-many-cats
94. <a href="https://www.freepik.com/vectors/minimalist-background">Minimalist background vector created by pikisuperstar - www.freepik.com</a>
95. <a href="https://www.freepik.com/vectors/cartoon-monster">Cartoon monster vector created by macrovector - www.freepik.com</a>
96. <a href="https://www.freepik.com/vectors/mercury">Mercury vector created by freepik - www.freepik.com</a>
97. <a href="https://www.freepik.com/vectors/monster-face">Monster face vector created by macrovector - www.freepik. com</a>
98. <a href="https://www.freepik.com/photos/bokeh">Bokeh photo created by jigsawstocker - www.freepik.com</a>
99. <a href="https://www.freepik.com/free-vector/brain-characters-cartoon-mascot-with-funny-face_8631175.htm#page= 10&query=aware&position=2&from_view=search">Image by upklyak</a> on Freepik
100. <a href="https://www.freepik.com/vectors/kids-clipart">Kids clipart vector created by brgfx - www.freepik.com</a>
101. <a href="https://www.freepik.com/vectors/meteor">Meteor vector created by macrovector - www.freepik.com</a>
102. <a href="https://www.freepik.com/vectors/summer-time">Summer time vector created by pikisuperstar - www.freepik.com</a>
103. <a href="https://www.freepik.com/vectors/pineapple-cartoon">Pineapple cartoon vector created by gstudioimagen - www.freepik.com</a>
104. <a href="https://www.freepik.com/vectors/summer-fruits">Summer fruits vector created by freepik - www.freepik.com</a>
105. Image by <a href="https://www.freepik.com/free-vector/set-funny-fruit-characters_1104776.htm#query=happy%20fig &position=19&from_view=search">Freepik</a>
106. <a href="https://www.freepik.com/vectors/winter-festival">Winter festival vector created by kjpargeter - www.freepik.com</a>
107. <a href="https://www.freepik.com/vectors/funny-food">Funny food vector created by pch.vector - www.freepik.com</a>
108. <a href="https://www.freepik.com/ vectors/cute-mouse">Cute mouse vector created by pch.vector - www.freepik.com</a>
109. <a href="https://www.freepik.com/vectors/city-life">City life vector created by storyset - www.freepik.com</a>
110. <a href="https://www.freepik.com/vectors/doughnut">Doughnut vector created by macrovector - www.freepik. com</a>
111. <a href="https://www.freepik.com/vectors/espresso-cup">Espresso cup vector created by catalyststuff - www. freepik.com</a>
112. <a href="https://www.freepik.com/free-vector/golden-laurel-wreath-red-round-podium-with-steps-front-curtains_24718530.htm#query=award&position=11&from_view=search">Image by Upl56</a> on Freepik
113. <a href="https://www.freepik.com/photos/sunset-sea">Sunset sea photo created by wirestock - www.freepik.com</a>
114. <a href="https://www.freepik.com/vectors/cute-mouse">Cute mouse vector created by pch.vector - www.freepik. com</a>
115. <a href="https://www.freepik.com/photos/coffee-table">Coffee table photo created by awesomecontent - www.freepik.com</a>
116. <a href="https://www.freepik.com/vectors/iridescent">Iridescent vector created by Olga Hmelevskaya - www.freepik. com</a>
117. <a href="https://www.freepik.com/vectors/light-banner">Light banner vector created by studio4rt - www.freepik. com</a>
118. <a href="https://www.freepik.com/photos/glitter">Glitter photo created by freepik - www.freepik.com</a>
119. <a href="https://www.freepik.com/vectors/tree-shape">Tree shape vector created by macrovector - www.freepik.com</a>
120. <a href="https://www.freepik.com/vectors/car-clipart">Car clipart vector created by brgfx - www.freepik.com</a>

121. <a href="https://www.freepik.com/vectors/magic-portal">Magic portal vector created by macrovector - www.freepik. com</a>
122. <a href="https://www.freepik.com/vectors/background">Background vector created by upklyak - www.freepik. com</a>
123. <a href="https://www.freepik.com/vectors/glow-line">Glow line vector created by freepik - www.freepik.com</a>
124. <a href="https://www.freepik.com/free-vector/comic-face-expressions-illustrations-set-eyes-mouth-cute-funny-angry-cartoon-character-emoticon-with-happy-smile-drawings-isolated white_20827600.htm#page=34&query=cute&position= 11&from _view=search">Image by pch.vector</a> on Freepik
125. <a href="https://www.freepik.com/photos/sunset-sea">Sunset sea photo created by wirestock - www.freepik.com</a>
126. <a href="https://www.freepik.com/vectors/colorful">Colorful vector created by freepik - www.freepik.com</a>
127. <a href="https://www.freepik.com/photos/wasting-time">Wasting time photo created by DilokaStudio - www.freepik. com</a>
128. <a href="https://www.freepik.com/vectors/mermaid">Mermaid vector created by freepik - www.freepik.com</a>
129. <a href="https://www.freepik.com/vectors/watercolor-background">Watercolor background vector created by kjpargeter - www.freepik.com</a>
130. <a href="https://www.freepik.com/vectors/magic-dust">Magic dust vector created by vectorpouch - www.freepik.com</a>
131. <a href="https://www.freepik.com/vectors/monotone">Monotone vector created by rawpixel.com - www.freepik.com</a>
132. <a href="https://www.freepik.com/vectors/glitter-effect">Glitter effect vector created by ilonitta - www.freepik.com</a>
133. <a href="https://www.freepik.com/vectors/amethyst">Amethyst vector created by macrovector - www.freepik. com</a>
134. <a href="https://www.freepik.com/vectors/laurel-crown">Laurel crown vector created by macrovector - www.freepik.com</a>
135. <a href="https://www.freepik.com/vectors/problem">Problem vector created by freepik - www.freepik.com</a>
136. <a href="https://www.freepik.com/vectors/hand-drawn-sketch">Hand drawn sketch vector created by freepik - www.freepik.com</a>
137. <a href="https://www.freepik.com/vectors/mice">Mice vector created by freepik - www.freepik.com</a>
138. <a href="https://www.freepik.com/vectors/background">Background vector created by upklyak - www.freepik. com</a>
139. <a href="https://www.freepik.com/photos/warehouse-worker">Warehouse worker photo created by senivpetro - www.freepik.com</a>
140. <a href="https://www.freepik.com/free-vector/retro-room-interior-vector-illustration_3076486.htm#query=cartoon% 20stairs&position=9&from_view=search">Image by vectorpocket</a> on Freepik
141. <a href="https://www.freepik.com/psd/nature-template">Nature template psd created by freepik - www.freepik. com</a>
142. href="https://www.freepik.com/free-vector/roulette-background design_1035696.htm#query=roulette&position= 2&from_view=search">Image by macrovector</a> on Freepik
143. <a href="https://www.freepik.com/free-photo/fighting-fish-black-background_13181446.htm#query=fish&position=41 &from_view=search">Image by tawatchai07</a> on Freepik
144.<ahref="https://www.freepik.com/freevector/kaleidoscopecolorfulbackground_800053.htm#page=3&query=kaleidosco pe&position =7&from_view=search #query=kaleidoscope">Image by dukepope.com
145. </a> on Freepik<ahref="https://www.freepik.com/free-vector/business-icons-design_1096018.htm#query=magnifying %20glass&position =11&from_view=search">Image by cornecoba</a> on Freepik
146. Image by <a href="https://www.freepik.com/free-photo/top-view-white-plane-green-background_14308174.htm# query =airplane&position=36&from_view=search">Freepik</a>
147. <a href="https://www.freepik.com/free-vector/set-silverware-isolated_11058463.htm#query=cutlery&position=4&from _view =search">Image by macrovector</a> on Freepik
148. <a href=https://www.freepik.com/free-vector/artistic-tool-seamless-pattern-paintbrush-tool-design-drawing-brush-pallette-craft-colorful-gouache-hobbywatercolor_10705373.htm#query=artists%20pallette&position=15&from_ view=search >Image by macrovector</a> on Freepik
149. <a href="https://www.freepik.com/free-vector/gemstones-background-illustration_2872086.htm#query=crystals% 20background&position=45&from_view=search">Image by macrovector</a> on Freepik
150. <a href="https://www.freepik.com/free-vector/symbol-consultancy-brain-logo-isolated-vector-design_24865799. htm#page=2&query=confusion&position=3&from_view=search">Image by Rochak Shukla</a> on Freepik
151. <a href="https://www.freepik.com/free-vector/three-roads-question-mark_10700620.htm#query=confusion&position= 43&from_view=search">Image by macrovector</a> on Freepik
185. <a href="https://www.freepik.com/free-vector/cute-animals-rainbow_20438329.htm#page=8 &query=animal%20 rainbow&position=47&from_view=search">Image by brgfx</a> on Freepik
204. <a href="https://www.freepik.com/free-vector/cartoon-wooden-isometric-chests-with-treasures_9166847.htm#page= 11&query=treasure%20chest&position=5&from_view=search >Image by valadzionak_volha</a> on Freepik
207. <a href="https://www.freepik.com/free-vector/expression-emotion-concept-set-cat-character-diffetent-animal-emotions_18779007.htm#page=2&query=cat&from_query=cat% 20angel&position=37&from_view=search">Image by jcomp</a> on Freepik
226. Image by <a href="https://www.freepik.com/free-vector/illustrated-english-prepositions-with-mouse_11754897. htm#page=2&query=mouse&position=1&from_view=search">Freepik</a>
228. <a href="https://www.freepik.com/free-vector/rate-singer-with-music-key-banner_30813828.htm#page=6&query =mouse&position=35&from_view=search">Image by brgfx</a> on Freepik
229. Image by <a href="https://www.freepik.com/free-vector/flat-design-crawfish-logo_22109626.htm#page=9&query =lobster&position=3&from_view=search">Freepik</a>
232. <a href="https://www.freepik.com/free-vector/cute-monster-cat-fantasy-alien-planet-landscape_28998018. htm#page=2&query=cute%20dragon&position=28&from_view=search">Image by upklyak</a> on Freepik
233. <a href="https://www.freepik.com/vectors/mice">Mice vector created by freepik - www.freepik.com</a>

www.ingramcontent.com/pod-product-compliance
Lightning Source LLC
Chambersburg PA
CBHW040859120626
46551CB00001B/91